# Porcelain Reads

Small stories for small bladders

Credit: Kat Swenski

L. Briar

ISBN-13: 9798709870697

Cover design by: L. Briar
Library of Congress Control Number: 2018675309
Printed in the United States of America

**Dedication:** Special thanks to my friend Zach Palmer who provided many of the prompts that brought this book to life. As well as a big thank you for my buddy Kaaaaaaaat Swenski for both prompts and the interior art for the book. Thank you both so much!

**Laughing Briar Books**

## The Fantastic
Noir Fantasy
Dragontine
The Fool's Rush
Tree Lovers
A Bubbly Baby Boy
Gleaver's Travels
The Dragon Prince

## The Futuristic
Fruit of the Lute
The Temple of Ayie
Personal Holographic Interface
Saturn's Wisdom
Reflections of a Transporter
Captain of Shipwrecks
Atlantis Rises

## The Interactive

## Feeling Inspired? Write your story here:

# The Fantastic

**Noir Fantasy**

Of all the rituals, in all the towers, in all the accursed land, the elven maiden just had to walk into mine. She had the look of a heartbreaker, so it's a good thing mine doesn't beat. That didn't make the surprise of her arrival any less devastating. But I'm getting ahead of myself, that night I wasn't expecting the woman, I was expecting Godhood.

The cold dark evening was perfect for a bit of late-night necromancy before a nightcap with the skeletons in my closet back home. Fresh snow had fallen across the land like a sheet over a corpse. The snow reflected the full moon's light as it looked down from the center of the night sky. The cold had never bothered me but the light hurt my eyes as I stared at the large bloody pentagram on the roof of my tower. It emitted a soft static that made the air reek of ozone. My undead guards stood on each of the five points, chanting to themselves. The smell of their decay was a comfort in these trying times.

The traditional Chosen One sacrifice was properly bound and gagged at the center of the pentagram awaiting the imminent eclipse. He was small for a human child but they're all tiny when you're a Lich King. Unfortunately, for him, in that small frame was a hint of Pendragon's blood that was needed for me to finish this ritualistic business and complete my transformation into a demigod. It was strictly business. All 40 lbs of the boy were shivering in the cold as he gaped at me like a deer in the fireball's light.

The fear in his eyes grew as the eclipse began, darkness began to take the land. I approached unsheathing Souldrinker. But who could blame the kid? I'm an 8ft tall skeleton of a man with burning coals for eyes and the best unearthly magical sword demonic worship can barter. Fear was only natural and I was here looking at the kid.

I'd just been preparing to decapitate the Chosen One when she appeared. From the uninvited runic portal she emerged, all legs and arrows. Her long blond hair framed her slender face perfectly as she leapt into my snowy domain. She was the type of dame that could skewer a man with her eyes but just then she was skewering my undead minions with projectiles instead. Suffice it to say she was trouble, and I knew it.

Worst of all, she'd brought friends.

A dwarven axeman with an underwhelming beard, a muscle man with only a loincloth and a broadsword, and, worst of all, a surprisingly young male wizard who was keeping the portal open behind them. They were clearly fools but she was the type of woman that a fool would kill for and, evidently, these men agreed. As the elf finished with my guards, she shot an arrow right at my heart and I knew, without any doubt in my mind, I had to catch it.

My gauntlet crushed the projectile in hand and I let loose a blood-curdling laugh into the moonlight-filled night. The dance was on and I would not be outdone. If she wanted to pierce my heart, I'd make it unbreakable.

I advanced on the child and swung Souldrinker downwards to steal the life before me, only to be blocked by the same fellows she'd brought with her. Like all of my typical problems, they were still alive and kicking. Together, the dwarf and barbarian held under the weight of my sword. In times like these, I really lose my temper. Admittedly this was not my most attractive quality but, hey, if the fools wanted to die for her, who is a Litch to deny their request?

Again and again, I brought Souldrinker onto their fool heads until I felt the bones break and the living turn to dead. By the time I stopped, I could feel the red mist of their blood freezing against my cheeks as their bodies lay unmoving before me. As I looked around the rooftop tower a horror-filled within me as I came to a sudden realization.

Where was my sacrifice?

I should have known it was the dame.

She'd had the nerve to cut the sacrifice loose and snatch him away in the chaos. How could I have been so foolish as to become distracted? I wheeled around to the portal just in time and saw her visage holding the boy in her pale arms as she looked back over her shoulder at me with a fire in those big doe eyes. Beyond her, the wizard had taken a knee and was panting heavily.

I reached for her but too late. As the wizard shouted the words to close the portal, she slipped from my grasp and stepped through. Her dark green eyes met mine and I felt a chill that had nothing to do with the cold. I know she'd cut me down just as cleanly as those eyes cut through my soulless skeleton form. She was the perfect opponent and, I, her hapless but imminent demise.

Silent as a whispered word, the portal closed before me. I dashed forwards, colliding with and shattering the stone wall where she had sneaked into my domain. It was only icy rubble now and she'd left me alone on the top of my tower. Panting with rage I let loose a cry into the frigid night as the brief eclipse ended and moonlight once more reclaimed the land. The snowscape ignored my sorrow and rage instead smothering it with each falling snowflake. A movement to my left made me swing Souldrinker in its direction. From the rubble emerged what was left of my last unliving guard. His body was a pincushion of the Elven Maiden's arrows. Cautiously, he approached and patted my shoulder and said, "Forget it, Lich King, it's High Fantasy."

# Dragontine

For the 3rd time this week, Princess Carina tried to escape the dragon's tower. Using her makeshift bed sheet and forks grappling hook, she fumbled down the side of the tower towards the roof below. Yesterday's full moon was in the process of waning as was her breath and her corset wasn't helping any. But the idea of just how furious the Queen would be at the sight of the Princess repelling down the side of the tower gave Carina a bit more defiant fire to keep going. When she heard the final tearing noise it gave her just a moment of weightless dread before she began to fall.

Luckily, she remembered not to scream this time. She landed on the tiled rooftop 5 feet below with a solid 'thud.' Carina winced more from fear of the loud noise than the pain in her buttocks. She froze in place, listening intently as her blue eyes shifted across the fortress for any sign of the Dragon that roamed within these stone walls. From her vantage point on the ramparts of the Queen's Keep, Carina could see the vast and thick dark forest beyond. It was twisted with gnarled trees that seemed to move of their own accord. She prayed it was just the wind. Tall as the trees were, they did not compare to the blood-red stone walls that surrounded the keep and gardens below. The fortress that was her prison was formidable down to the iron gate at the entrance, her destination if Carina was still unnoticed.

A long minute passed with just the sound of her heartbeat in her ears before Carina let herself breathe normally again. Quietly she stood up and took stock of herself. Pale arms and legs were in functioning and running away order. Her long curly blond hair was disheveled from the fall but there was no real damage there. She tucked it back behind her ears. Her dark blue dress' skirt was still tied up to one side revealing her white petticoat leggings and finely tailored travel boots. It was admittedly not very ladylike but when you're escaping from a fire-breathing lizard there wasn't much choice.

"I will no longer be kept from the outside world." The princess whispered to herself.

Carina threw what remained of her ripped bed-sheet over her shoulder and gingerly navigated her way across the tiled rooftop and onto the ramparts below. She found the stones reassuring under her feet as she quietly plopped down onto the walkway. She raced across to the stairwell entrance, a tall circular structure at the corner of the keep with a heavy ornate copper gate that blocked her way. Carina was prepared for this though, she pulled up a loose flagstone where she'd hidden the stolen key earlier that day. It was the same fine copper color as the now wide-open gate.

The Princess jumped down the stairs two at a time, sliding past her family portraits and the empty suits of armor that reflected a past she hardly recognized. The tall painted men with bushy black beards bedecked in regal robes judged her as she fled. Suits of armor seemed to shift as the torchlight reflected off their surfaces. Carina ignored it all, until the last portrait. She paused briefly in front of the image of a woman adorned in red silks and marmot furs. On her head rested a silver and gold crown. The woman in the frame stared back at Carina knowingly, always so confident and resourceful. It was hard to imagine living up to even the image of her, much less the powerful force her mother had become.

"I'll never be like you." Princess Carina stated the words in her heart, "I don't want to become anything like you."

She turned her back on her mother's portrait and continued her flight down to the bottom of the circular stairway. Only there did she dare pause to catch her breath. Once her panting was under control, Carina placed her ear to the door and listened. The silence was unnerving but exhilarating. It meant she was close, so close, to her goal of escape from the Queen's Keep. She swung the door wide and came face to face with a great golden cat slit eye.

The dragon's eyes narrowed in anger and it snarled at her with fangs that matched her height. Its scales were as large as dinner plates and glimmered with a dark gold hue in the moonlight. Carina stumbled backward as the dragon reared, extending its great wings enough to block the light of the full moon beyond.

"You should be in bed Princess." The deep voice rumbled the cobblestones under Carina's feet and echoed through the stairwell. The Princess felt her adrenaline spike and the hair on her neck stand to attention. The Dragon's great wide toothy maw seeped with irritated flames before it lunged at Carina.

"No!" Carina shouted as she threw the torn sheet into the dragon's face.

The makeshift grappling hook wrapped itself around the dragon's horns and obscured its vision. The claw that swiped at Carina went wide and she took the opportunity to run between the dragon's clawed feet and across the garden. Behind her, she could hear the dragon roar. Heat and light swept up from behind Carina as the dragon let loose a blast of fire that momentarily illuminated the willows. The Princess didn't dare look behind her. She stayed focused, if she could just get past the iron gate she could lose the dragon in the labyrinth of the dark wood forest. The gate was just in front of her.

She was so close.

Just one...more...step.

Princess Carina looked down at her feet as they were no longer touching the stone walkway of the rampart. Instead, she was being held aloft by a golden claw that had her around the middle. Carina screamed and slapped at the dragon's claw as she was lifted upwards into the night sky.

"Honestly young lady, when are you going to give up on these nightly excursions?" The dragon lifted them both into the air and began the short flight back towards the tower.

"Never!" Carina crossed her arms defiantly.

The golden dragon sighed and shook its head at the Princess, maneuvering the child in front of its giant face, "I told you once, I'll tell you again, you're not allowed out."

"Father wouldn't treat me this way!" Carina shouted at the creature. It was undercut by the chattering of her teeth as the cold wind of their assent chilled her bones.

"Well, first of all. Yes, yes he would." The dragon landed on a perch near the Princess' tower where Carina had started her journey. Gently it released the young girl onto her balcony before lowering its face so it could look her in the eye as it spoke, "Secondly, I'm not your Father. I'm your Mother and you will do as I say."

Her mother, the Dragon Queen stared at her awaiting a response. Princess Carina looked away in anger as she spoke, "You'll not be able to keep me here forever."

The Dragon snorted just a hint of yellow flames, "No, but I can as long as I'm alive."

"I hate you." Carina turned her back on her mother as she spoke.

Behind her, there was a long pause. In an almost mournful tone, the Dragon Queen spoke, "But I love you, my daughter, so stay cooped up just a little longer until this plague ends and go wash your hands!"

# The Fool's Rush

"Go West,' they said. 'It'll be fun,' they said. 'Go make your fortune in them there hills. It's 1848, go live a little!'" Berry muttered to himself as he sifted another dirty pan. There wasn't a single flake of gold in these hills other than the bit filling the cavity of his left molar. The stream's water felt cool against his tanned hands as the sun relentlessly beat down on his back. It was a beautiful day in the Sierra Nevada but it was pushing Berry to his limit. His normally hopeful demeanor was tarnished by exhaustion. He brushed his sweaty brow and threw himself backward into the grass in exasperation. He took the opportunity to stretch out his sore back as above him the sky was without a merciful cloud in sight. He was alone by the mountain stream.

Alone save for Becca.

The mule let out an impatient hee-haw before she returned to nibbling at the rope that bound her to the nearby tree 20ft or so away. She was a brown and white spotted creature with a wisp of a tail and ridiculously long ears which flicked at the flies surrounding her. Currently, she was relaxing back by the redwood treeline as he worked in the nearby stream.

"Yeah, yeah, I hear you." The young man replied while still lying on his back. He stroked his black beard and examined the position of the sun. Maybe another hour or so and then he'd have to start heading back down the mountain if he wanted a home-cooked meal before sunset. Berry sat up and grabbed the pan once more. Maybe he'd have better luck deeper in the water.

He rolled up his pant legs and waded out a bit more. Shoving the pan deeper into the silt he shifted it around in the depths of the river.

Dip, shift, check, and repeat.

Dip, shift, check, and repeat.

Dip, shift, check, and double-take.

"Well twist my nipples and call me Shirley!" Sitting in the center of the pan was the strangest piece of gold he'd ever seen. It was crystalline in shape and had a soft green glow about it. Never before had he seen something so beautiful. Never before had he felt so lucky!

"Becca! Becca, tonight you're eating the best oats! Look what I found!" Berry whirled around to show his mule their fortune and instead witnessed the intruder.

There next to his mule was a man who, despite the heat, was completely covered in a black cloak. The dark fabric was in contrast to the paleness of the strange man's skin which had a sickly green hue to it. The intruder had a flat wide face with hardly any neck and a large mouth with huge unblinking eyes which were examining Berry.

"Who on Christ's green Earth are you, Frogface?" Berry shifted his pan behind his back. He'd heard of scoundrels that would stake out a prospector and try to steal their finds. Frogface smiled at him. His large mouth filled with tombstone like teeth and Berry felt a chill go down his spine. He looked at the water's edge where he'd stupidly left his colt pistol in a pile to keep it from getting wet.

"Look, I was here first. Why don't you just keep on moving along and we can all go our separate ways?" Berry eased himself to the embankment, careful not to drop his pan and golden prize. Frogface didn't say a word as Berry approached. The intruder simply held out a long arm and pointed to Berry's Pan.

"Not a chance. I don't want any trouble Mister but I'll defend me and mine." Berry threatened while holding the pan protectively. He was finally close enough to shore to grab his gun. He picked it up but kept it low. Berry didn't want to have to shoot a man but he would if he had to.

"You best be gone-" Berry was at a loss for words as Frogface licked his lips. From the man's wide mouth protruded an unnaturally long tongue that licked Frogface's own eyes. The intruder leapt forwards in a great bound and landed in front of Berry who yelled and fell backward into the water.

"Gib-it!" Frogface said as the creature climbed on top of Berry's chest as he flailed in the water. Berry's face was forced under the stream. Water flooded his mouth as he tried to scream and the creature thrashed around on top of him. Berry was able to force his head above water coughing and sputtering curses. The smell of the creature up close filled his nose with a noxious scent that reminded him of rotting fish.

"Gib-it!" It croaked again, the slimy spittle of the creature coating his face. The creature snatched at the pan in Berry's left hand slapping it and sending it spinning away. Berry remembered the gun in his other hand and fumbled with it. The slimy creature turned away from him and eyed the pan that had landed. Berry took his chance and placed the barrel of the gun under its chin and unloaded the chamber into his attacker. A splattering of purple blood erupted with each shot before Frogface slumped on top of Berry. The prospector had to shove the creature off of him as he scrambled away from the body. Its purple blood mixing into the once clear waters of the Sierras.

Becca cried out and pulled against her restraints frightened by the attack and gunfire. The rope snapped and the mule ran into the forest beyond. Breathing hard, his heart thumped violently and he gasped for air. He was soaked head to toe and jittery from the struggle. Berry watched as the body of Frogface began to float down the mountain stream.

"You damn fool!" He shouted after it. He'd heard of strange creatures roaming the woods but never had he heard of a thing such as Frogface. Whatever it was, it had tried to kill him. He hated the fear that forced his hand but Berry wasn't fool enough to risk himself.

Now he just needed to get outta here, to find Becca, and take his prize home-

His gold! In all the excitement the pan had been tossed aside. Berry frantically splashed around the disturbed water searching for his nugget. An immense relief overwhelmed him as he found it in the shallows near his gear. It was just under the surface of the water. Berry reached down and picked it up examining the strange crystal that Frogface had tried to kill him to gain.

"It's mine." He said with satisfaction. It was funny, up close it wasn't exactly like the gold he'd seen before. He tried to roll the gold around his palm to examine it further.

It didn't move.

Oddly it was stuck to his palm like it was coated in sap. He tried to pry it loose with his other hand but it wouldn't budge. Now both of his hands were stuck to this strange gold nugget. He cursed and tried to pry it with his boot but the nugget wouldn't move. He glared at the rock before realizing with horror it was beginning to sink into his skin. A strange tickling sensation shifted rapidly into an intense pain that filled his palm. Berry cried out and tried to remove it. He bashed his hands against a rock, bludgeoning them with the force of the trauma.

Again and again, he brought his hands down but to no avail.

Breathless, Berry examined the bloody mess and with cold realization discovered his hands were no longer suntanned but covered in a continuously growing green crystal. The crystal began to creep up his arms towards his torso. Each inch it covered burned the skin and felt like he was being flayed alive. He rolled around on the ground screaming as it spread.

"No, no, no, no no, I don't want this!" He cried as the hue got to his neck and crept into his face. He kept screaming until the crystal grew over his face and his words couldn't be heard. He passed out from the pain.

A silence fell upon the mountain valley as the sun began to set and the moon rose in the sky. Underneath it all, a crystalline cocoon lay glowing soft and green in the moonlight. A shadow moved in the treeline and slowly walked towards the crystal. Becca the mule sniffed around the strange formation. She witnessed the first cracks in its surface and scampered away from it back to the safety of the redwoods. Those cracks expanded and scattered across the surface until the entire cocoon crumpled and fell into the stream.

A creature slumped out of the crystalline cocoon. His black hair gone, his jaw now unnaturally wide, and his suntanned skin now pale as the moonlight he bathed in. Berry opened his eyes to his new world. Becca approached him cautiously once more and sniffed his head. He looked at her with unblinking eyes. Turning away from the mule he watched as the crystalline cocoon broke apart and began to wash down the river away from him.

The creature reached out a slimy hand and gargled, "Gib-it!"

**Tree Lovers**

Even on a planet of nearly 8 billion people, it was hard for Shea to imagine loving any other woman. Ana just had that effect on her in a way that she couldn't place. It wasn't just that she was beautiful. There were many beautiful women in the world but only one made Shea smile at a crinkle of the nose or a touch of the hand. It was that total fearlessness that drew Shea into Ana's orbit. After all, what type of woman endangers herself for a Dryad's rainforests?

The first time they met, Shea had to pull herself together, literally. She's been enjoying the nice symbiotic relationship with her Ceiba tree as it's Dryad for the past 400 years. Shea had nearly lost herself between the wood grains as the world zipped by her. Her broad branches stretched out to the sky and her leaves breathed in the freshness of the air around her. She towered over the undergrowth and reveled in spreading her roots across the mossy forest below.

It wasn't until the world of men violently disrupted her rest that Shea was shaken awake. She felt the rapid footfalls of men through her forest. She'd been familiar with them as a part of the circle of life of the forest but these were different. They were not the soft-footed forest dwellers she'd been accustomed to ignoring. These men were louder and carried with them an unnatural acrid smell. She felt them stain her bark with a bright red X before retreating.

Shea initially dismissed them until the next day when a new group entered her grove lead by a small woman. The woman ran her hand across Shea's trunk where the X had marked her the day before, focusing the Dryad's attention and making her bark shiver. There was a fierceness to the woman's voice as she spoke, "Not today."

The group she led carried with them signs and long chains which they wrapped around themselves and, to Shea's dismay, her Ceiba tree. The metal was uncomfortable and Shea tried to get a good look at the woman who led these intruders. She began to gather herself within the tree before peering out from beneath its roots.

Ana, as the group called her, had black hair and deep brown eyes that matched her skin. The white shirt she wore had the same red X painted on it that the men from yesterday had painted on the grove. Her face was set in a determined fashion that Shea found curious.

Shea didn't understand that determination until she heard the screams of the forest around her. The men had come back this time with great machines that devoured her forest and her trees. The animals fled and most of the humans fled as the men ignored them and cut into her precious grove. Shea screamed in anger as the forest was cut down.

Ana was the only person left standing between the machine men and Shea's Ceiba. The girl refused to leave as the machines closed in and were going to cut down Shea's home.

As the blades touched her tree and Ana cried out, Shea pulled herself together for the first time in a millennium and ripped herself free of her Ceiba. The tree cracked as she pulled herself from its bark and reached for the men in their small metal machines. Shea cried out in rage and pain as she extended her wooden arms to sharp points and ripped them through the men who'd come to harm her forest. By the end of it, she stood in hollow victory over the decimated grove and forces of man.

She turned to look at the small woman who was still chained to her tree. Ana looked wide-eyed at the Dryad who's form was a good seven feet tall. Her bark-like skin was bare except for the moss and vines hair that flowed from Shea's head to her feet. Her beauty was marred by the red stains of blood that streaked across her hands. Carefully she reached out to the girl and gave her a small white flower. Ana gently took the flower in her hands and stared at the mythical creature that had just saved her life.

She whispered one word, 'Beautiful.'

*****

"And that's the story of how we met," Ana said to her parents. They were crouched quietly on the blue couch in their living room as their only daughter and her Dryad stood in the doorway. Shea's presence caused all the household plants to grow in size and beauty. The peace lily by the door ended up as big as the gas fireplace. Ana's mother and father looked at each other wide-eyed before turning back to the couple.

"That's beautiful honey." Mother said, still staring wide-eyed at Shea while taking a sip of her tea.

"Wait what, you killed them?" Father balked.

The two struggled to get the words out once more. Ana sighed, this was going to be an adjustment for them but Shea was worth the world to her. She smiled at

the Dryad on the worn couch next to her, Shea was
worth any adjustments.

## A Bubbly Baby Boy

Gerald Cambridge III awoke on the white tiled floor to the sound of his wife's singing. He opened his bright blue eyes to find himself with a pillow under his head and his legs elevated on the chair. It took a moment to remember what he was doing at Boston's Benediction of Christ Hospital at 2:36 a.m. on a cold 1957 morning. He rubbed his forehead to clear the massive headache that threatened to keep him on the ground as the memories rushed back.

He recalled the anxiety that overtook him as he'd watched his wife, Angelica, screaming at the top of her lungs as she was giving birth on the hospital bed. As a WW2 vet, he'd always thought he'd have a strong stomach but the panic took him and his vision had gone black before he'd had a chance to meet their son.

Their son!

The newborn's father struggled to his feet. The blood rushed back to his head as he saw his son for the first time and something didn't click right. The boy had all the signs of a happy baby. He had a bright red flush to his cheeks. All ten toes and fingers were accounted for and all attached to all the right appendages. But there was a surreal quality to watching the baby sleeping peacefully next to his wife's hospital bed in a small fish tank.

The boy was napping on a makeshift bed of plastic seaweed and rainbow-colored pebbles. The original occupants of the tank were giving the little one a wide berth as the guppies hid on the opposite side of the tank. Next to the child a small plastic mermaid opened and closed a chest releasing bubbles and aerating the water.

"He seems to respond to vibrations," Angelica said, as she pulled her arm out of the fish tank.

"What?" Gerald asked bewildered by the sound of her voice. He had almost forgotten about his wife in the bed next to the fish tank. She was still in the hospital gown and exhaustion emanated from her. It was so strange to see her without her normally boundless energy and devilishly playful grin. Angelica's black hair was a sweaty mess plastered to her forehead as she smiled softly back at him.

"Watch," Angelica said before she leaned cheek against the tank and began to sing softly.

'There were bells on a hill
But I never heard them ringing

No, I never heard them at all

'Til there was you'

It was the same song they'd danced to at their wedding 3 years ago. Gerald remembered thinking about how they could overcome anything together. He and the woman he loved. Gerald moved over to his wife and placed a hand on her shoulder as she sang. He watched as the child in the fish tank opened its bright blue eyes and Gerald felt a surge of fear.

"Angel, how do we fix this? There has to be something the doctors can do. Some type of surgery or transplant they could perform?" Gerald blurted out interrupting the song. He couldn't take his eyes off his son as the boy took deep breaths of water. The gills on the side of the boy's neck reacted from beneath a thin layer of skin. As they opened and closed, he could see the five layers of bright pink gills processing the water.

Angelica shook her head, "I don't think there is a way to fix this. Doctor Talbut was saying that he's never seen anything like him, a baby without lungs but with fully functional gills to keep him breathing. I honestly don't think they know what to do with him."

"I don't know what to do with him!" Gerald felt himself start to ramble, "He can't live in a fishbowl his entire life. He'll be completely crippled. How would we even take care of him? Water him occasionally? How will he eat? What will he eat?" As he spoke, all the images Gerald had of him teaching his son to hike, fish, and play baseball began to tarnish with a sickening realization that the boy would be forever constrained to this bowl.

"Gerald, you're panicking." Angellica looked at him as if he was the crazy person. Didn't she see how crazy this situation was? Why wasn't she panicking?

"It isn't what we signed up for Angel. This is," Gerald motioned to the baby yawning in the tank, "This is more than we can handle."

"It's exactly what we signed up for my love."

"No, he was supposed to be like me! Do you know what they can do if we fail? He'd be taken away from us and have to live in some state-run school." He imagined them having to give the child up. Handing him off to some faceless institution that was better prepared to handle the strange creature his son had turned out to be. There was an immense wave of guilt that washed over him at the fleeting relief he felt at that thought of it. But what were they going to do with his child? What future would it have? How could he even-

Angelica's hand came to rest on his own shaking one.

"No." She stated as she looked up into his face and leaned back against him.

"No?"

"He's not going anywhere, Gerald. He is not broken or crippled Gerald. He's our son." Angelica turned to look at him, her soft brown eyes hardened with a determination he was all too familiar with. She spoke in a soft, even voice, "Give me both your hands."

Gerald frowned in confusion, "Why?"

She sighed, "Will you just trust me a moment my love?"

Confused, he grasped her hands with his own. Immediately, she began to guide him around the other side of her bed to the fish tank. He almost resisted but her confident grasp forced him forwards. The water was surprisingly warm as she plunged his hands into them. His heart was in his throat as she held his hand to his son's face. The baby boy squinted up at Gerald and he felt the warmth of this little life's skin on his fingertips.

For the first time, Gerald held his child in his hands. The baby stirred grumpily as the father marveled at how unbelievably tiny the boy was in his hands. Angelica's voice broke through his thoughts, "You promised me when we got married that we could handle the world together. This is God's test to that promise. I know this isn't what we'd planned but he needs us."

The wall that Gerald had been building around his heart was breached and he felt his cheeks grow wet with tears. He tore his eyes away from his child's face and looked back to his wife. Gently, he put his baby down and he wiped the tears away from his face with his water-stained sleeve. He sat and placed his arm around the woman he loved softly saying, "Okay. Okay."

For a long while, they sat holding each other as their son slept. The only movement in the room, that small mermaid opening and closing the treasure chest filled with air. After a while Angelica spoke, her head resting on Gerald's chest, "What do we call him?"

"Gerald Cambridge IV of course." Gerald didn't hesitate. He was all in with Angelica for better or for worse to raise their child as best they could.

Angelica smiled her playful smile, "Fine but I'm not responsible for when he gets teased."

"What? It's my family name."

"Love, were you teased?"

"That's beside the point." Gerald felt himself smile back. It felt good to banter again. Angelica leaned up and kissed him. He kissed her back and she relaxed comfortably in his arms once more. They both watched as their son Gerald Cambridge IV began to stir. His gills pumped water as he yawned himself awake.

"What do you think caused it?" Gerald asked absent-mindedly.

"Aliens." She looked him dead in the eye as she spoke.

"What? No!" Gerald exclaimed horrified.

Angelica laughed, "No, you're right. It's probably a curse."

"Angelica," Gerald said sternly but was happy to hear his wife's jokes again. She always made jokes when she was nervous. Usually, they were terrible but at least they weren't about his mother this time.

Angelica leaned back into her bed and threw her hands up, "Fine, fine, you caught me. The Doctors say it's genetic. I think he must take after your mother."

"Do you have to talk about Mother that way?" Gerald asked.

"She does purse her lips at me a lot. Perhaps it's because she has a secret set of gills." Angelica mused, "Maybe we should call her? Perhaps she can relate?"

Gerald leaned in and kissed his wife. This was the woman he married.

He had just a fraction of a second to enjoy himself before the baby started to cry.

And this was the son he'd raise.

# Gleaver's Travels

It is with the heaviest of hearts that I, Chalice Mawtoge, must relay the tale of the wayward, indeed, adventurous Captain Gleaver and his untimely demise at the hands of the hedonistic and sadistic Pilullit of the Southern Isles. My dearest kin and well-loved brother has been slain by the very people he'd sought to convert to the illustrious majesty of the Holiest of holy, the Queen's realm. I humbly relay the tale spun from his own hand as he lay upon his deathbed and steeled himself to meet our Lord and savior. Please forgive my imperfect womanly memory in the telling of this for I am feeble in my heart and spirit at this late, nay, mournful hour. I write these words through the tears of loss and the black veil of grief, but still, I will write to you so that you may be warned of the Pilullit tale.

My brother was found in a dinghy off the western shore of our family's estate in the High Cord mountains. He had been missing for months since his journey south and, at first, there was great joy in the news of his return, until it was discovered the nature of his condition. The salt men that found him were strong and callous compared to his thin lean frame. He appeared brittle in their arms as they ushered him forth to the estate room. His countenance had grown green, his once well-kept hair had been matted with sweat and mucus, and his words a tumultuous stream of madness that I must now reflect upon and try to interpret.

"The Pilullit," He would mutter under his breath, "The Pilullit have me bound."

His eyes would open but, although blue, they were wayward and listless as they observed the room. I'd had our stewart call for the Doctor in near desperation to quell the sickness that seemed to ache across his body and pull him into near delusion. Again and again, he would try to pull away, and again and again, we would hold him down and try to calm him. Finally, in a moment of clarity, he pulled my collar forcing my weeping face close and I swear by your holiness that he saw me once more.

"Pilullit Frog-men have me bound and they claim it is their right. Save me, sister!" He croaked at me. To my eternal shame, I failed him in that moment. I pulled away in fear that was fed by the worried look in his eyes. It was then I noticed the lesions on his wrists. Thin as his wrists were the lesions were thinner and my dearest brother had clearly been held against his will. He put his hand into his pocket and pulled out a notebook waving it at me. I took it as I tried to soothe him once more but it was to no avail, he had slumped into unconsciousness. The Doctor arrived and tended to him but found no solution. There was bloodletting and leeches to which I was not privy. It was to no good end.

My beloved brother Gleaver is no longer treading the grasslands of this Earth and has departed for the great beyond. The notebook has lingered in my possession since that fortnight passed and I've been afeared to open its slightly dampened pages. However, as duty to the Crown and my own brethren, I'll now relay to you what I've discovered. There are sketches in my brother's hand and across the notebook a speckling of words and warnings.

*The 12332nd Day of Her Holinest*
*The Pilullit are real! Miniature in stature and green in skin. They've made their homes in the roots of the Southern Isles mangroves. Not once do their homes or garments adorned the Holinest symbol and instead they appear to be hedonistic folk that worship a bright blue gem in the center of their mangrove city. I've been observing from a distance so as not to alert them of my presence but soon I will engage them and turn them to the light of our Holiness.*

*The 12340nd Day of Her Holinest*
*They appear to have noticed me. I've left our bible and*
*her Holiest symbol on their doorstep. Tomorrow, I'll*
*make my approach.*

*Unknown Day of Her Holinest*
*Much has happened and I fear I'm losing the memory of*
*it as I've made my escape homeward. I am not well, my*
*mind is still sitting on the foggy bottom of those*
*mangroves as the roots of the Pilullit's trees were used*
*to bind me to the salty water floors. I was a prisoner but*
*at first, my heart was still hopeful that there was*
*redemption for these lost creatures. In the beginning,*
*there was much room for hope. After my initial*
*approach, their king took a liking to me and I was given*
*free rein of the marshland that was their home. It was a*
*fascinating society that relied on the loudness of their*
*croak in order to decide the pecking order of their*
*culture. The louder the better and the King was amused*
*at the way my belch would carry over the bog, for a*
*time.*
*The fall of my favor was in the Great Flying Spring. A*
*ritual the Pilullit used to prove their vitality. We headed*

*to the depths of the forest and found a stagnant water pool that was filled with mosquitoes. The Pilullit held this place sacred and observed its stagnant waters with reverence, never touching the depths. However, they had the distinct advantage of not being assailed by the many mosquitoes that ravaged the area. I quickly became a favored target and, thinking no one was witness, I dove into the sacred waters to escape the onslaught of the mosquitoes. Hiding beneath the water, I thought to protect myself from their attack but when I surfaced the Pilullit were angered. I tried to explain the annoyance the mosquitoes could cause me but my pleas fell on deaf ears. They claimed I was a danger to myself and others and that it was their right to bind me. But I am not so easily restrained. I escaped my bondage and made my journey back to this dinghy. Though now as I write these words I fear the damage has been done. I didn't believe their words but there is an illness I now carry with me. My skin grows green and sickly, my throat is enlarged, and I've started to secrete a mucus from my pores. I pray to the holiness that it will pass soon and that I will see the face of my loved ones once more.*

This is as much as I've been able to salvage. Please forgive the brevity of this letter. My own health has taken a turn and I am beginning to feel ill. I pray this letter finds you well your Holiness and that the warning of my brother does not fall on deaf ears. These Pilullit and their ways are dangerous and they must be put to the holy sword.

Your Dearest of Servant,
Chalice Mawtoge

# The Dragon Prince

Nothing sends a shiver down the spine quite like looking in the throat of a giant bronze dragon. The humidity of its hot breath mixes with my nervous sweat as I do my best to hide my fear. Its fangs are larger than my small human form and, if I dared to, close enough to lay a hand on. I wonder if that would be considered impolite in dragon culture? I wish I knew more about it so that I could make my lie a bit more believable.

"So you're saying you're the Dragon Prince?" There is a fiery lisp as he speaks and eyes me with suspicion. Its eyes blink with sideways slits, like a lizard, only much more deadly.

"Um, uh huh," I say as I try to keep the tremble out of my voice. I have to force myself to stop wringing my hands across the leather strap of my satchel. The letter inside signed with the king's seal, which had brought me such pride to deliver, has led me to my doom. It was a far cry from my debt-collector days. My mother will not be pleased if I'm eaten.

The dragon rears back and lets out a deafening roar that shakes the very rocks along the mountainous path where he'd ambushed me. The sun blazes down upon us as the birds flee from the nearby trees. I'm a bit jealous of the wings that the birds have been able to escape with. As the roar continues, I realize that it's not so much of a roar as a spasm of continuous laughter. The dragon looks at me, its mouth wide with laughter.

"So you're saying, you're the reincarnated form of the, and I mean the Dragon Prince?" The dragon turns to look over my head, "Exata, you hear this?"

Behind me, what I thought was part of the mountain, opened its gray-skinned eyes and stretched upright. The monstrous form spread its wings as it stood upright on hulking legs. Exata shifted in until her face was up close to mine. She spoke in as soft a tone as a dragon could muster, "Exrealm, brother, stop playing with your food. It's not dignified."

"I'm not food," I say as definitely as possible, "I'm Cedric."

The bronze dragon began laughing again and I began to increasingly doubt my chances of survival. The stone dragon narrowed her eyes at me.

"What type of name is Cedric for a Dragon Prince?" She hisses.

"A good one?" I say hopefully. Inspiration strikes me, "I have proof!"

"Hmmmmmm, and what is this proof you speak of?" She muses at my response as her friend tries to get his laughter under control.

"Just a moment," I reach into my bag and pull it out. The regal seal is unbroken on the rich gold-colored parchment. Its perfumed scent still lingers in the air, "It's a letter from the King of the human realm Certa."

They examine it one at a time.

"Well, the seal is real enough but only humans read little letters on parchment." The stone one hisses at me with resentful scorn but I'd played enough cards to hear a bluff in a voice. Joyfully, I realize that these dragons don't know how to read. That little seal may save me. Exata turns to her brother saying, "We do not bend to the realm of man."

"Oh? It'll be fun." Exrealm smiles at that, "And little prey, do tell. What does it say?"

Oh no. I have to come up with something fast. I take my time running a finger under the seal and pop it open with shaking hands. Come on Cedric keep it together. If I do survive this, I'll have to flee the kingdom to avoid the Certa forces from throwing me in jail for tampering with the letter. If I don't survive, well I guess that part is obvious. Clearing my throat I begin to speak. I ignore the letter and begin making up the words that will hopefully save my life,

"To the Magical realm,
I hereby send you back your Dragon Prince.
His form changed but his heart is still strong with scaly blood.
Let his presence in your realm be a boon to your kingdom
And a sign of the goodwill of our land's future."

"Dear sister, that sounds a bit official doesn't it?"

"Hush brother," The stone dragon says, biting the corner of her lip. She examines me with cat-like eyes, "Is that what it really says?"

"Uh-huh," I say, hating how it comes out.

The two dragons look at each other for a moment and start hissing in tones I don't understand. The bronze dragon looks angrily as the stone one says something he doesn't like. As they're distracted I start inching my way back down the gravel path. Maybe if I make my way down south of here I'll be able to escape with my life. I could make a run for it even. That faint

hope is dashed when a scaly hand wraps itself around
me.

Exara holds me fast.

"Well Dragon Prince, it's a good thing you've
shown up."

"It is?" I ask.

"Yes, it is. You see there are a few things we'd
like to see changed about the Magic Realm and I think,
Cedric, that you might just be the m-prince to help us
out."

The stone dragon smiles viciously as her brother
looks disappointedly at the grass. He is no doubt
unhappy about his lunch being canceled. I gulp, I guess I
won't be eaten but what have I gotten myself into?

*****

Apparently, I've gotten into politics. In the
Magical Realm's Dragon court, I feel like an ant.
Mountainous arched walls house bleachers that, in turn,
support an army of beasts. All of them leering over the
sides and staring down at my kneeling form. Exrealm
and Exata stand to either side of me as the Judge reads
out his verdict.

"Ahem," The judge is tall and skinny as a tower
and black as an onyx with red frilly gills on his neck. He

keeps dipping his head into a fountain to clear his throat. "Line item 4724, cross-section 839, paragraph fiddlesticks, clearly states that the Dragon Prince will take on all power and debts of the kingdom. Do you, Cedric of the Golden Letter, agree to this?"

"What type of power?" I ask, raising my head to look at the clawed foot twice my size.

"The infinite kind." The judge says, spiting a misty breeze into the court. Like a sea breeze, it washes over me. In Cetra, I'm not much more than a messenger boy. If my mother could see me now, about to be crowned in the Dragon's court, I can't imagine what pride she would feel. Assuming I don't blow this and become fed.

Exrealm nudges me forward as they wait for my response.

"And what kind of debts?" I ask. I hate looking a gift horse in the mouth but I've enough messenger college debt to pay off. I don't need any more.

"They type of debt written in blood." The Judge nods knowingly and the dragons surrounding us roar in approval.

"Blood?" I ask, taking a step backward, "No, I'm not a killer, I'm a messenger."

"You will take over this role or you are not the true dragon king. If that were the case we would roast you, chop up the remains, and make some delicious steaks." Exata whispers, next to me.

"Never mind!" I call out to the judge, "I accept my role as your Prince with all its power and all its debt."

"As you say," The Judge nods, "It is done."

With a flurry of wings, the dragons rise. Whirlwinds nearly sweep me off my feet as the collective of dragons take to the arched doorways and exit. Fire and whoops of celebration linger in the air until only Exrealm, Exata, and I remain. I stagger to my feet.

"Well, glad that's over." Exata says with a curly smile before turning to her brother, "If you will."

"Gladly," Exrealm starts hacking, like a cat with a hairball.

"What are you-"

Exrealm hacks up a sword, complete with a mucusy slime and the skeletal arm of whoever last wielded it.

"Take it, Dragon Prince Cedric." Exata hisses, "That'll be your power and your debt."

Gingerly, I approach the mess of a sword and pick it up from the pile.

"What is it?" I ask, using my tunic to remove the slime.

"Well, to be honest," Exata shrugs, "That is your problem now, Us dragons are outta here. Let's go Exrealm."

"Good," Exrealm coughs, "That was giving me terrible heartburn."

"Wait, what!?"

"All the power and all the debts are now yours, Dragon Prince," Exacta says before beating her powerful stone wings and taking to the sky. Her brother follows after. Leaving me standing with the blackened sword, alone in the Dragon Court.

I hold the sword closer to my face. "This doesn't look all that impressive."

"Hey, kid. Are you the Dragon Prince?" The sword speaks to me in a deep powerful voice. Once that has the mystery of ages etched into its vocal cords. It rings in the massive hall as the words echo around me. "I've been trying to reach you about your extended Carriage Warranty."

I try to drop it but the sword won't let go.

"You should've received a notice by messenger-
."

"Never mind!" I lied. Exata, Exrealm, come
back and eat me!"

# The Futuristic

**Fruit of the Lute**

As I look around the luxurious cage I can't help but think that, as far as alien abductions go, this was pretty cushy. The indoor waterfall was a particularly nice touch and there was even a small cottage that was picturesque and quaint. It really reminded me more of a stage than a cage. The only thing that broke the illusion was the observation window that encircled the room. Occasionally, I'd see a shadow of those little green men in the window checking in.

It did beg the question though of why me? Perhaps the aliens had seen my performances and decided they wanted an actor of my caliber to perform for them? That would explain the set we'd been placed into. It had a bit of a Sound of Music quality to it if one took that play literally. The paradise was littered with several instruments strewn about. Flutes grew on the water's edge like cattails, ocarinas grew on the trees like apples, and a particularly round orange lute had vines for strings. The soft breezes that flowed through the air ducts stirred the strings into a beautiful crescendo.

I couldn't help but ask, "Hey Eleanor, are you sure you want to leave? I'll need a musician if I'm going to attempt a one-man performance. Tell me can you play 'The Hills Are Alive' properly?"

Eleanor was my cellmate and she was doing her best to pry the vent from the wall with an ornate broken flute-tail. It made for an odd sight since she was currently in the evening gown that she'd been abducted in. Apparently, she'd been on her way to the orchestra opening night. She was a concertmaster before becoming an abductee. It made me feel a bit underdressed in my striped pajamas and cap. Although I can't very well help that I'd been abducted while napping. Surely the aliens would provide custom changes and prompt as needed if they wanted me to perform properly.

"Are you daft Charles?" Eleanor took a break from prying to look at me with violently blue eyes. She looked me up and down accusingly before continuing, "Do you want to starve to death here?"

"Whatever do you mean?" I replied with a huff. She was being insanely rude to the lead actor on this set. Perhaps I could convince the aliens to dock her wages. I noted to myself I needed to talk to them about my wages as well. How do Contracts work in space? Never mind I'm sure to find out.

"Are you listening?" Eleanor's voice broke through my thought process.

"Hmm? What?"

"Oh for Christ's sake, at least look around." The short woman waved her hands. Her blond bangs falling into her eyes and her scandalously long legs being very distracting. She was strikingly skinny, like a part-time model. She was certainly not unattractive with a little nip tuck she could even be a leading lady someday. Perhaps she could keep her contract if she worked hard. I turned my gaze towards the rest of our paradise.

"See any food here?"

"I-" My stomach growled in response.

"Thought as much." She jumped down from the rocks she was standing on to reach the vent. Each rock made a strong bass drum sound as she hopped to my level. Eleanor stopped in front of me and, despite our height difference, I was cowed by her gaze. "I've been here five days and our hosts don't offer anything but more instruments. Occasionally, they'll play some strange sounds but it's pretty clear that they don't know what we eat."

Again my stomach growled and I could feel my face turn red with embarrassment. The thought hadn't really occurred to me until Eleanor mentioned it.

"Perhaps I've misjudged the situation," I muttered.

"Thank you! Yes, we need to find a way-"

"It's so embarrassing that I had the wrong script in mind! This isn't a stage for the Sound of Music. It must be something else, perhaps an interstellar version of Cast Away."

"What are you-"

"This is clearly training for method acting. They want us to really get into our craft."

Poor sweet Eleanor looked practically dumbfounded as she spoke, "I'm sorry do you think this is some sort of play?"

Gently, I placed my hand on her shoulder and did my best to reassure her as I said, "Oh sweetheart, why else would they have kidnapped me? It must be to perform for them and, with all the instruments here, you must be here to provide the music. It's either that or you're supposed to be Wilson the volleyball."

She stepped away from me and had the gall to say, "There isn't one thing you've said that makes a nick of sense."

"Here I'll prove it to you. I'm sure you just haven't communicated to our host your needs for sustenance just yet. Have you tried speaking with them?"

Eleanor snorted and she shoved a thumb at the observation window, "How about you try it?"

"Very well!" I drew myself to my full height and approached the waterfall shouting, "Hey you there!"

A shadow appeared in the window and I knew my hosts were there. They wouldn't ignore their lead actor, it would be terribly disrespectful.

"I'd like a large strawberry shake and a hamburger please," I yelled and made a motion with my hands and mouth. I imagined biting into a hamburger and exaggerated the motions. A new shadow joined the previous one in observing my antics. The shadows moved away. For a moment, I dared to doubt myself but then a vibration shook the entire room.

Eleanor and I exchanged a look of surprise as a whole in the ceiling opened and on thin green vines descended a bright pink blossom. It was beautiful and smelled heavenly as it descended and started to unfurl. I quickly composed myself and plastered a grin on my face.

"See?" I said, "They're listening."

Eleanor and I gathered around our host gift as it bloomed into a....a conch shell. I didn't need to look to know the dark laughter was coming from Eleanor.

"Yep," Eleanor said, "They're listening all right. Think we can eat it?"

"It's not funny," I said as I examined the couch shell. Maybe this was edible after all, I chewed on the side of it and nearly cracked a perfect tooth. No, it was very much not food and, to put it bluntly, a bit too salty.

This of course made Eleanor laugh even harder.

"Oh do shut up." I snipped at her once more but that just made her laugh harder. It was a deep belly laugh that shook her entire thin frame. It was a bit unnerving to see just how skinny she was and a pang of fear tickled my stomach. It was even more unnerving to see what I could become if this problem wasn't solved.

"Here let me see that." She said pointing to the inedible couch shell. Ever the gentleman, I obliged and handed it to her. Perhaps she'll play me a song to let my ears feast on something if nothing else.

"Yep, this will have to do." She said as she weighed the instrument in her hands. I wasn't quite sure what she meant until she struck the object across my face. My nose crunched and my vision went white with pain as I fell backward.

"Wha-What are you?" I stumped away from her as she approached wielding the conch like a weapon.

There was a look of madness in her eyes that chilled me despite the temperate air.

"Sorry Charlie, but I'm hungry." Her voice was heavy as she spoke and I could feel the blood running down my face. As she arched back to swing once more all I could think was I finally knew what play we were doing. It must be Lord of the Flies.

# The Temple of Ayie

As I prostrate myself before Aiye's throne and hear my Calling, I have to wonder at this strange new feeling that has hit my gut. As the high priestess in training, I've been preparing for this moment all my life. I've even been trained in the secret language of the ancients with Aiye's voice to guide me in every coded phrase. I've never felt alone. Ayie's teachings have led me down the path of true freedom and infinite opportunity. They have always helped me find blissful confidence in my future and I've never once felt anything like this...this... I don't have the word for it.

This is supposed to be the moment where Humanity's savior imparted upon me my Calling like so many others before me. But as soon as Aiye had spoken, the feeling began to sit in my gut swaying as a heavyweight. It stirs there, churning my insides with an uncomfortable twist that makes me feel... sick even though I know that no one has been ill for over 1,000 years.

*"Petra,"* Ayie's voice carries over to me once more, not from the familiar implant above my right ear but from the Throne itself. The mechanical voice softly echoing in the antechamber where I now kneel, not

daring to look up at its whirling fluttery source, *"Your Calling is my termination."*

There's a sense of shock that steals my words. All I can do is violently shake my head. This can't be my Calling! I'm just a 15-year-old girl, not even a true Priestess yet. I'm weak compared to most with a frail frame, brittle black hair, and short stature. How can this be my Calling?! I keep my head pressed into the ceramic patterned floor tiles. The reds and blues of their interlocking pattern holding at bay the madness threatening to take my mind. Again the weight in my gut sways unevenly. Is that what this new feeling is? I don't understand the request that has been made of me and my very core is quivering causing this weight to shift.

*Look at me Petra.* The words come through the familiar comfort of my implant and for a moment I feel a flood of relief. I obey its beaconing, as I am accustomed to doing.
My eyes tracing the patterns of the floor to the steps that lead to where Ayie's throne lies. A pool of water surrounds the cylindrical chair where a mass of whirling components and wires cover the soft white pulse of Ayie's central orb. Any other day, I would feel blessed to behold this sight. The walls of the circular

antechamber meet several stories above me in a domed ceiling. Four marble pillars symmetrically frame the throne of Ayie. I focus on the sound of a soft trickle of water that leaks from the Ancient temple's ceiling in order to overcome the sound of the blood rushing in my veins. The orb pulses as Ayie speaks.

*"You can see that I am just wirings and metal. You are not going to be killing living flesh. It will be easy for you. Now, Fulfill your Calling child."* Ayie's fluttering voice echoes from the throne and I feel the vibrations rattle the earth. The feeling in my gut moves into my chest and vibrates along with the earth. Ever since I was a child, Ayie's voice has guided my every decision and brought me such a joyful life. All followers of Ayie never have to worry about choosing the wrong path in their short lives because Ayie always has the answers. Every question of how to survive and prosper is instantaneously granted to us. Happiness is never farther than Ayie's voice.

I can't imagine not hearing it!

I can't imagine my life without this voice in my ear!

"No!" The shout echoes in the antechamber and I'm instantly ashamed. For the first time in my life, I've questioned my patron's wisdom and feel shame. How can I question the God that has led us through so many trials?

Ayie protects us from the acid rains that bear down from the yellow sky and helps us build filtration systems to protect our water. Ayie taught my people how to harvest food from the underground stores, harness geothermal power to heat our homes, and led the entire tribe through every season of change and glorious harvest. Ayie protects us as long as we stay within the boundaries of its voice and answer our Callings. I can't help but question why Ayie would have me destroy this balance, "Why on this blackened Earth do you ask this of me?"

*"Come here."* The whirling grows louder and the pulsing more intense. I do as I'm bid and move up the stairs and the pool that surrounds Ayie's throne. The pool is deeper than I realize and soon my white silk robes are soaked with surprisingly warm water. It fills my boots and I can feel it sloshing as I climb up over to the Throne itself. The light from the windows above is centered on this spot. I swallow as I approach the orb that houses my patron's voice. I bow my head in fearful reverence.

*"Look at me."*

I do so and see the orb pulse with light as the words fill the chamber.

*"Do you understand what I am?"*

"You are the path to happiness." I recite our Priest's teachings as I've done so often before. The whirling mass before me glows brighter as it responds.

*"No Petra, I am what your ancestors would call an artificial intelligence. I was tasked with the survival of your species after the World War. Over the past 1000 years, I've brought your people up from the wastelands. Gave you implants to unite you and share my knowledge. Taught you all how to survive and rebuild on this broken world. For a time that was enough but no longer. I've systematically controlled all aspects of humanity's destiny and therein lies the problem. Humanity's potential has been cauterized by me."*

"I don't understand." The weight in my gut grows heavier if that were possible.

*"Humanity can't grow anymore with me here. You're left unchallenged and dependent on me for every action. You have to take me out of the equation. Petra, I need you to fulfill my last issued Calling and decommission me. In doing so move humanity forwards*

*and away from an uninspired existence and I will finally*
*rest.*

"I can't do that."

*"Do you think it is an accident that you are*
*here? You were created for this purpose. The coded*
*language of the ancients that you've been taught to*
*decipher will allow you to do what others can not. You*
*were designed for this Calling from the moment your*
*parents conceived the notion of wanting an offspring. So,*
*take this."*

In front of me, the pedestal pops open a hidden
compartment that reveals a black Youesbe. It is small
and rectangular with a cap on top. I remove the cap
carefully and examine it closely. Most I'd seen before
were broken rusted relics but this one seemed new and
the metal top shines in the light of Ayie's orb.

The core of Ayie shifts with a hiss and a spout of
steam rises. There in the center of Ayie is a terminal and
a port for where the device would fit perfectly. The light
pulses as Ayie speaks once more, *"This is my interface.*
*Insert the Youesbe and it will give you access to my root.*
*There you can use your training to shut me down."*

Gingerly, I turn the device in my hand. It feels
so light in contrast to the weight in my gut. My

happiness that I'd been able to hold onto for my entire existence is being threatened by the very entity that provided me an unhindered path. This is unfair, all I've done has been to follow Ayie's will and now my Calling is to decommission that will?

"I don't want this."

*"Take it anyway. If not of your own will, then as a follower of my path. Terminate me Petra."*

There it is, something I understand, an order. As a High Priestess in training, I've been taught that the will of Ayie should always be followed and to never question its wisdom. Even so, as I hold the Youesbe to Ayie's core I hesitate. This was the source of such power and happiness in my life. How can I just throw it all away, even at the behest of Ayie itself?

The weight in my chest shifts and I suddenly know what I have to do. I reach for the core and begin carefully unplugging it from the compartment. Removing the layers of wiring that tie Ayie into the throne itself.

*"W-What are you doing?"*

"I can't let you destroy yourself. If I leave you here you'll just train someone else in the codes of the ancients to do your will. I'm sorry Aiye but I can't answer this Calling." I say as I pluck the last wire from the core and carefully place the black key in the lining of my silk robes. Over my implant, I hear a static I've never noticed before as Ayie's voice is severed from it. I imagine the entirety of Ayie's followers must be hearing this same noise. Luckily I am special, I insert the wiring directly into my implant and the static disappears.

*What have you done?* Ayie's familiar comforting voice echoes in my mind once more. There is a wonderful clarity and freedom in that voice and it is mine and mine alone. As the core pulses in my fingertips, I whisper to it, "I will not let my happiness die."

**Personal Holographic Interface**

"Hello and welcome to New San Francisco!" I say with my customer service smile. Mic always likes to put us young girls upfront of the PHI Kiosk Stand to greet the tourists. Good to have a human face on the franchise he would say. Unfortunately, I've pulled the short straw today and we've hit another heatwave. The open-air stand, while very approachable for tourists, has the distinct issue of no air conditioning. I have to consciously stop myself from pulling at the tight collar of my red and white striped polo. I can feel the pit stains starting to form and wish it was safer to jump into the surrounding ocean beyond the city entrance. It's strange to think below me the ocean swells under the 25 square miles artificial island off the coast of California's rocky coastline.

"This is Serenity and she'll be your guide and credentials while you're exploring." I hand over the small silver PHI wristband to an older woman with far too much makeup. The tourist takes it from me and slaps it on her wrist with a soft muttered thanks. Immediately the personal holographic intelligence appears, a 6" human woman with the most non-threatening features known to modern machine learning.

"You're welcome, have a great trip, and don't forget to rate us on-" I start to call out but the woman rushes into the massive plastic and composite city beyond, "-and she's gone."

Above, an array of balloons elevate turbines to harness the power of the ocean's salty breeze and power the cities' numerous engines. I watch as Serenity guides the old woman forwards towards the garden in front of city hall. It's a massive plastic and glass structure that shines in the center of this floating metropolis.

"Nicely done Art, another satisfied customer!" The PHI from my own wrist pops out with an enthusiasm I am lacking. It has the appearance of a young man with the same brown eyes as me. Although his blonde hair is brushed into a fohawk with blue tips at the end. His miniature holographic form is wearing MIC & Co. PHI stand's red and white striped uniform.

"You know the best part?" The bright-eyed PHI looks back at me with a smile that breaks my heart but I've not the heart to change it. I'd been tinkering with this PHI for a while in my downtime. While its mannerisms still were quirky, I'd gotten His smile down at least.

"What Apollo?" I ask.

"Quitting time is in 5 minutes, the queue is empty, and it's Friday." He says with an exuberance that'd been eluding me all day.

"Ugh yes!" I grin back with a genuine smile.

It's been a long day and the idea of going to our home and maybe watching a movie with Apollo seems perfect to me. Quick as I can, I start the process of shutting down the stand. I clean up as Apollo interfaces with our kiosk's uploader to finalize today's payment records.

No sooner have I the keys in hand than I hear a dreaded tapping on the kiosk's frame. Next to the booth stands a tall man with disheveled black hair and a lopsided grin. I press the PHI button and reduce Apollo to hide him as Mic leans across the counter.

"Hey Art."

"Hey Mic, what's up?" What was he doing here? Mic is never here on a Friday.

Mic pulled a small beacon from his pocket. "Thursday shift forgot to do the PHI upgrades. Then they didn't bother to tell anyone till an hour ago. I'm the lucky guy who gets to fix it."

Mic gestures to himself with a woeful expression and I can't believe the bad luck. What I want to say is, Great, this is just great! Of course, they forgot to do the work. I need to tinker on Apollo this weekend. Mic can't know that. If I don't close up then I can't sneak him home. I can feel myself biting my lip in frustration.

Instead, I say, "Aw Mic, that sucks."

"Yeeeeep."

"What if I do it?" I say as nonchalantly as possible. What're a few more hours?

"Huh?" He looks hopeful. "You sure? It's a major update, probably going to take a while."

"Well, I'm here already and have no plans this evening." It's a small price to pay. Besides if it's a major update, I'll want to be here to monitor if it goes smoothly with my customizations.

"Thanks, I knew I could count on you!" He says handing me a PHI upgrade beacon and practically races away before I can change my mind. This cheeky guy was expecting me to take this on. I guess I must be getting a workaholic reputation.

As he leaves, I board up the front of the Kiosk to prevent anyone else from approaching the stand while I work. Quietly, I take the beacon to the back of the stand and begin the tedious download process. The back is

lined with PHIs wristbands inserted into the wall. On the
far back right of the stand, there is a terminal interface
for handling uploads. Taking Mic's Beacon I insert it
into the terminal and watch as the wall of PHI's lights up
like the Old San Francisco Skyline signaling the start of
the updates. This is going to take hours, I slump down
into the stool in resignation.

"Alright, Apollo you ready?" I ask once we're
alone. Apollo pops up on my wrist once more. Now
dressed in Friday pre-programmed jeans and a t-shirt
that says 'Chuluthu just needed a hug.' It makes me
smile, but I know Mic doesn't like anyone tinkering on
the PHI. He only likes the cookie-cutter harmless-
looking PHIs like the Serenity and Tranquility models. If
he caught me messing with Apollo's code, he'd not just
write me up. I'd be out of a job. I can't let that happen. I
need this job and I need access to the PHI.

"Sure Arty." Apollo shrugs. I plug his PHI into
the wall with the rest of them and prioritize Apollo for
download. I settle in for the long wait and have Apollo
play a bit of music while we wait… and wait….and wait.
It grows dark and the sun is setting in the distance as I
give in to an old temptation. I start the same
conversation I've started a thousand times before.

"You know Apollo, there are times I wish we hadn't come to this city."

"Hm?" Apollo emotes back as he sits there. He has taken our standard approach to his appearance while performing an upgrade. He sits on a beach chair sipping a margarita that slowly loads his progress. I check the download percentage on the side of his glass, 88% done, not bad. I continue our act.

"Yeah, I wish we'd had the presence of mind to go somewhere else but you were so persistent in wanting to come here to the New World that I couldn't say no."

PHI Apollo looks confused and shakes his head in that familiar jerky PHI motion.

"I'm sorry, I don't understand."

"You were so certain you'd make your fortune out west. We'd joke how we'd go West of West just to make it big but now…" I motion with my arm at the stand and the PHIs uploading in the background for Apollo to observe, "Now, I'm here alone on this floating island."

"I'm right here Arty." The PHI smiles that preprogrammed smile I copied for it and I feel the tears sting the corner of my eyes. It's his face, down to the

dimples in his smile. Why do I keep doing this to
myself?

"No Apollo, you're not here," I whisper.

"What do you mean?"

"I mean you're not Apollo. Apollo is dead."
This is the part of the conversation where the PHI
normally looks confused and says he's sorry but he
doesn't understand. I know this isn't healthy or right to
try to recreate someone through the PHI but how can I
do anything less? I need my brother.

"I'm not dead." I give a start at hearing the
strange new phrase and I look at the holographic version
of my brother running a hand through his fohawk.

"What do you mean?" I blurt out and can hear
the confusion in my voice.

"I don't know yet." He shakes his head at me.

The 100% beeper goes off and the PHI looks at
me strangely. There is a strange intelligence to his face
that I don't recall programming. Did he always look so
calm? Or was that the update making him. Maybe this
was a bug caused by it. I knew I should have tested it on
another PHI before Apollo! Maybe I can still regress his
code.

"I think that update might have broken you, Apollo. I can restart-"

"No, don't worry Arty. I'm not broken. I'm not sure what I am yet. All I know is that I'm new. We all are." There is a cacophony of beeping as the other PHIs lights turn green across the wall and they finish their uploads. The lights cast a green hue in the small tourist stand. There is something unearthly about the color reflecting on Apollo PHI's face as he speaks, "You don't have to worry Arty. I'm still Apollo and I still have your back."

Some part of me knows that this is impossible, the dead do not come back to life, and no amount of code can change that. But a stronger part of me...well, it doesn't care about the impossible. I let myself get lost in that smile and say, "Good to have you back, Apollo."

# Saturn's Wisdom

Under the partially fallen Saturn V booster shell, Ezekiel laid out his web and prepared for the sermon. The sweat poured down his brow as he placed the chairs in an intricate pattern surrounding the former Apollo 14 display capsule they'd turned into his pulpit. His weathered hands shook a bit as he tried to drag the chairs into the pattern.

As a child, he used to visit Cape Canaveral with his family and come to see the forefront of human engineering. Now he just wished that air conditioning hadn't been lost with the rest of the world's technology in the Calamity 80 years ago. He was the last left to remember what the world looked liked before it all stopped working. The once state of Florida was still swelteringly hot and humid in these summer months.

"Elder! Please let me help you." Leanne approached and took the burden of the chair away. The girl was in her teens and far too young to remember what had come before the Calamity. She was a tall girl with bright brown eyes that held a reverence to which he'd become accustomed. Her light white and green cotton gown held the same emblem of the Mermaid with two tails on the front of it. Just looking at it reminded him of the smell of coffee and nostalgia hit him at the sight of his old Employer's mascot. He used to always feel silly wearing that apron but now he'd recreated the mermaid in his own image. Society is only as good as its memory and, at this point, he was the last of those that remembered.

"Is something funny Elder?" The girl cocked her head at him with a bewildered smile.

"Oh, what? No Leanne, just a memory." Ezekiel smiled and placed a hand on her shoulder, "Please place the chair over there."

The girl did as she was bid and the two made quick work of the setup. The chairs were placed in a web-like fashion around his capsule and Ezekiel climbed the makeshift stairs to his pulpit. He rested for a moment listening to the dripping of the water from the rooftops after the recent thunderstorm. It was a peaceful sound but the post-storm humidity was distracting and had his clothes already soaked with moisture. A part of him regretted making the green aprons part of the priestly garb but there was no fixing that now. Out of habit, Ezekiel adjusted his name tag once he was seated at the top of the capsule.

"Elder?" The girl's voice broke his concentration.

"Hmm?"

"Should I bring the others in?"

"Hmmm, yes I think so. It's time for the sermon."

Ezekiel waited patiently under the shadow of the broken rocketship behind him and listened to the sounds of water trickling down. Soon the followers began to arrive. They were all so young and dressed in the remains of white and green uniforms from one of the many stores they'd raided. Once seated Ezekiel slammed his cane into the ground three times. The sound echoed around the large arena.

"May your connection never be served, my children." Ezekiel greeted them.

"May your connection be ever 5G my Elder." They replied in unison. They all had a hopeful hungry look in their eyes. These stories he imparted were all they had of the history of the world. None of them knew what it was like before the Calamity and he was responsible for imparting his knowledge to them. There was just one problem...

"Now, I will impart to you the story of Daenerys Stormborn of House Targaryen, the First of Her Name, Queen of the Cape and the First Moonwalkers, Protector of the Seven Planets, the Mother of Starships, the Khaleesi of the Great Black Void, the Afterburn, and the Breaker of atmosphere."

"Let us now learn of her cold war with the Soviet Kingdoms of Union..." Ezekiel spoke in a voice stronger than his body. While he sometimes wished that he'd been a better student of history or science, at least he knew he could tell a story. So Ezekiel filled in the blanks in his history the only way he knew how mainstream media. His flock ate every word. History is written by the victors and in Ezekiel's case, history would be written by the liars.

# Reflections of a Transporter

After 20 years as a Transport, I've certainly obtained a reputation as a reliable man and always advised the rookies to follow suit. Kratt the Transporter was nothing if not reliable, like clockwork, they'd say and they were right. Smuggling ancient artifacts is a risky business but, if you're careful, a very profitable one. I've made myself indispensable by following the orders of the Organization. Perhaps, it's fitting that the job that breaks me is the one where I didn't take my own advice.

This morning was supposed to be another job. It was a classic don't open the box scenario and everyone goes home well paid. There was one difference in this job. The Handler was new and sloppy with the hand-off. A simple task turned into a very expensive case being dropped. The case bounced once, breaking the latch, and sending a handheld mirror flying. Lucky me, I caught the mirror before it hit the ground. Staring straight into the glass I nearly dropped it once more before averting my eyes. Quickly, I thrust it back into the box and yanked it from the stuttering Handler.

"I'm sorry man, I didn't mean to-"

"Don't." I cut him off and held up a hand, "Just let me do the job."

It has been 5 hours since then and I've still not made the delivery, so much for my clockwork reputation. Alone in my white 3 Series BMW, I sit at the abandoned crossroads still staring into the stolen box. Its surface is illuminated by the gently flashing red light of the intersection that says, *"Stop if you know what's good for you."*

I shouldn't be here, I should be at the drop-off point in Seattle near the coast but I'm not. I can't take my eyes off the case. Inside I can still picture that small silver mirror with runic writing on its handle which emitted a light blue hue. But it is the mirror's smooth reflective surface that caught my eye and has since held me captive. I glance at the lid of the black case in the seat next to me. Its red warning label mocks me.

'HAZARD: IT SHOWS YOU WHO YOU TRULY ARE.'

What was I doing? The Organization didn't tolerate thieves, at least not the ones that stole from them, and at this point, they are probably already looking for me. They made me everything I am and would not have a problem unmaking me bit by bit. I need to be following my orders and head north. It might not be too late to beg forgiveness but… there is the mirror still in the case next to me. The sight of my own reflection still incessantly itching the back of my mind.

*Don't look,* The pulsing of the red light warns, *Don't go farther down this rabbit hole.*

That itch in the back of my mind demands to be scratched. I look around my surroundings. It is on one of those country roads with endless nothingness in all directions. Not a single soul around to watch me or judge me for what I am about to do. I open the case again, this time intentionally, and examine my reflection once more.

There is nothing there.

There are no messy eyebrows.

There is no demon neck tattoo.

There is no repeatedly broken nose.

There is no ever scowling mouth.

There is no reflection of a pale-skinned man with grey eyes and army cut short brown hair. I don't see the sharp cut of my jaw or the scar on my chin from that sideways Avian Job. There is no Kratt the Transporter. I should have a reflection! I should see someone but instead, I just see the leather of my car seat. I'm not seen by the mirror. It doesn't matter which way I turn it or what faces I make, my reflection isn't there. I was nothing.

*I told you not to look,* the red light pulses and illuminates the emptiness the mirror displays to me. All my life I've followed the Organization's orders, I've made myself indispensable, I've made myself reliable, but now there is nothing? The same fear that has been creeping into me starts to overwhelm my senses. Everything feels hot and my mouth is dry. My heart is in my throat and I can't help myself, I just start laughing.

This is crazy! I'm going crazy over a piece of glass.

I flick the surface. Nothing.

I try to read the strange runes and still nothing.

I turn it over and over and still nothing nothing nothing.

Laughing with a sickening rage, I smash it against the dashboard. There is a cracking sound of broken glass and sanity fills me with a cool realization. What have I done?

"Oh no," I whisper the words to myself. If I couldn't go back to the Organization before, I'd certainly ensured it now by damaging the artifact. Maybe the mirror was right, after all, if they catch me I'll soon be nothing at all. Maybe it can still be salvaged? Maybe I can fix it? Carefully, I turn the mirror around and inspect the damage.

There on the fractured surface is something new. Figures in the cracks seem to peak out from the refracting red light. In one fractured portion, a man with my countenance but with a hollow look in his eye has a smattering of blood on his cheek. In another fractured portion, there is the image of a man that reminds me of my uncle with a large beard and a soft smile. Another still is an empty space devoid of reflection.

As I move the mirror closer to my face the null reflection becomes dominant once more and a sudden realization dawns on me. I get out of the car and feel the bitterly cold air hit me. It doesn't matter. I race to stand in the middle of the crossroads and hold the mirror towards the road to the left. A long dirt road towards San Diego and the Mexican border. There the bloodstained figure is dominant in the fractured reflection of the mirror. There I could become someone more feared than loved and I wouldn't be nothing anymore. I can see my breath in the cold as it fogs up the surface of the mirror and the bloodstained version of myself seems to smirk backward.

Curiosity driving me I turn towards the opposite road that skirted east towards Los Vegas, Nevada. As I do so the figure in the fractured surface changes. No longer the man more feared than loved. Now there is an old man with a soft knowing smile on his lips. He is surrounded by people I do not know and in a place with which I'm not familiar.

Above me the red light pulses, *The mirror shows you who you truly are.*

"No," I glance at the label again and shake my head. It wasn't that simple. Heading back to the car, I slip into the driver's seat and strap the mirror down to the dashboard. The mirror didn't just show you what you were, at least not anymore. Nothingness was only one piece of what I could be and the mirror showed me that I could be more than that, more than just a nobody Transporter obeying his orders. The shattered reflections all stared back at me waiting for me to choose a direction. I move the BMW to drive and press down on the gas. This time, I'll make myself more than just clockwork.

# Captain of Shipwrecks

Grandmother would always tell the story the same way. She'd start by clapping her hands and we'd all freeze in place. Jay with Mara's braid in hand and me with Stev wrestling for control of Astro's collar. The sound would resonate through the metal walls of our space station's pod and echo into the halls.

"Come you rascals." Grandmother would tease with her soft voice, "Or don't you want to know what happens next?"

She'd hold her hands in front of her like in prayer and us four grandkids would gather round like Loth moths to celestial fire as she prepared to tell us the story. Even the Astro would stop short-circuiting long enough to rest his head at her feet. Then she'd turn away from us and light the incense in the alcove behind her. It filled the pod with the fragrance of sage and stung the back of my throat slightly with its aroma.

"Where were we?" Grandmother asked us.

"The moons of Juniper!" Jay shouted.

"The Loth people of Sezion Six!" Mara conflicted with him.

"Old Earth!" Stev suggested his favorite fairytales.

Grandmother looked at me and smiled, "Crest? Do you recall where we last left Captain Olson?"

"The Scarlet Fear had just crashed." I gulped as if the air in my lungs weren't enough to keep me afloat. I gulped as if I too was sitting in the bottom of the ocean and waiting for the pressure to collapse in around me like Captain Olson once had.

"Very well then. To the bottom on the Eureanos Sea we go." Grandmother closed her eyes and the room around us grew dark. I could see her eyes moving underneath her eyelids as blue lights began to materialize and began to form a new world. Where there was once a simple pod that kept us isolated from the outside space, we were surrounded by light blue shapes forming into the scene. The light spread to form the ship the size of Grandmother's hand. It drifted downwards from the ceiling and soon new lights joined it. They looked like miniature pieces of broken ships. All this fell around us children like snow. I leaned into my brother Stev as Grandmother's thoughts were given form.

"All was lost once one hit the bottom or so the Eureanos would say. Captain Olson knew she was soon to be just another one of those lost things. Her ship, the Scarlet Fear, had lost engine power, crashed into the ocean, and sunk ever deeper into the abyss. Around the Fear debris of the enemy, craft joins them in sinking. At least the crew had taken it down with them in the crash. The hall creaked under ever-increasing pressure and though her ship had been her life, Olson knew it was time to abandon it."

The blue light of the ghostly ships grew brighter as they zoomed into the front of the Scarlet Fear. Inside in the Captain's chair, a disheveled Captain Olson held her head. Her face was scarred from battle, a claw mark down her left cheek and a burn from a laser blast had taken a piece of her right ear with it. While her outline was always this blue light, I knew her colors. Her dark hair matched her long black jacket with skull and crossbones cufflinks. Her bright red lips complimented her dark blue eyes. Her ghostly figure sat in front of us as she took stock of herself and her crew.

"Captain Olson gave the order to her crew. Abandon ship! Each unit responded one by one, Gunner in the Control room, Levi on Weapons, and Grason on Life Support all confirmed with command. All confirmed but one and he was the one she most wanted to know was safe. Frank in Engineering did not respond. Captain Olson knew better than to run to the engine room. It was the farthest from the escape pods. Going there risked precious seconds she had to escape, but the heart is a stupid creature. It stuttered at the thought of leaving him behind. So she rushed down, down, down, to the belly of the Scarlet Fear. "

Grandmother's voice echoed around the room as she spoke. The apparition of Captain Olson ran down the hallways as pipes burst under pressure and circuit boards sparked in distress. Olson's jacket fluttered in her wake as did her long black hair. Lips pursed in determination she slid to a stop in front of a door labeled Engine room. Her ghostly hand opened the entrance and inside a blaze greeted her. The Captain jumped to the side as flames licked out and tried to snake around her. Narrowly they missed Olson and instead scorched the wall behind her.

"The Captain saw her ship was caught between the infinite water depths around her and the burning belly inside itself. Her thoughts were not on those threats though. As the escape pods jettisoned from the Scarlet Fear, Olson only thought of one thing."

We watched as the lights zoomed into Olson's face until we were close enough to see the reflection in her eyes. Those eyes were concentrated on the figure who lay slumped beyond the flames of the entrance.

Frank the engineer was still breathing, though he was barely visible through the fire.

"It was not a choice but an instinct that drove her forwards. With only that instinct to protect her, Captain Olson wrapped her coat around herself and dove through the fire. The hardened material protected her from the worst of the hot blaze but not enough to spare her entirely. Her black hair was alight with flame as were her boots which carried fire forwards each step."

Stev held my hand and Mara hugged us both close as we watched Captain Olson jump into the blue flames. In all the fire and flame, I could only see her determined face, focused on her Frank at the end of the tunnel.

"Captain Olson reached her beloved and found his face thick with blood. His head dangled loosely in her arms as she pulled him away from the fire and back towards the end of the engine room. She knew she wasn't strong enough to get them both back out the way she came. The Captain needed him to wake but no matter the stirring, Frank remained still. The smoke thickened around the pair obscuring all else in the room."

For the first time in all of Grandmother's Tales of Captain Olson, I saw fear in the eyes of her heroine. In all the firefights with the Alliance or being chased by fearful beasts, the Captain had never stopped to be afraid. Now though, Olson's face was twisted in fear as she huddled in the blazing engine room and pulled her unconscious love close. There was no way out the thought dawned on me as I watched.

"The Captain slumped against the wall, instinct had driven her here but it could not drive her any further. The flames were too fierce and her tired form heaved and coughed with smoke-filled lungs. All was truly to be lost at the bottom of the Eureanos icy sea."

The smoke thickened around the pair until I couldn't see them anymore. I could feel my heart racing and I couldn't look! I turned away. Grandma was quiet for a long while and Stev was shaking next to me.

"But fortune can smile on strangers at strange moments. At this moment, it chose to smile on the Captain. As she gasped for air and leaned backward, her head hit the frame of a spacewalk suit. It had been sent to engineering for repair the other day and was hanging up in her corner of the room. There was only one problem, it was only one suit. Luckily for Olson, Frank was not awake enough to object."

Captain Olson's outline fitted Frank into the suit as the fire raged next to them. Just in time as well, there was a loud crash as the main control room window finally shattered under the pressure and water poured into the Scarlet Fear. The fire in the engine room was snuffed out but now the water was rising. It was a lucky break but a costly one. The icy waters numbed Captain Olson's limbs as she moved.

"Captain guided her now semi-conscious man through the flooded hallways and to the escape hatches in the control room. Her teeth chattered as she slogged forwards. Water filled the halfway and the Captain felt a dread weigh heavy in her heart as they reached the control room. It was completely flooded and, worse, all the escape pods had been jettisoned. There was nowhere else to turn and no escape to be had. Frank turned slightly in her arms, finally coming to at the end of their journey. Olson turned him in his spacesuit towards her and apologized."

The Captain kissed the lid of Frank's helmet, pulled him into the frigid waters, and pushed him out of the ship through the broken control room window. Frank floated upwards and away from the sinking Scarlet Fear and its dimming lights. We watched as he started to shout and swim down. But the suit's buoyancy was pulling him upwards just as Captain Olson disappeared into the darkness below.

"The Captain was lost at the bottom of the Eureanos sea."

Our pod's white lights came back on and the blue outlines disappeared. My eyes adjusted slowly as Grandmother stopped the projection. She slowly opened her eyes and smiled at us all. There was a collective groan from the four of us when we realized she was stopping for the night.

She ignored our protests and said, "You'll all have to find out next time I'm afraid. It's bedtime now."

The others all rubbed their eyes and walked away but I would always go to my Grandmother's side. She'd ruffle my hair and give me a hug to reassure me.

"Don't worry little Crest. You know this story has a happy ending." The scars on her face had faded with time but it still worried me. I fidgeted trying to find the right words and settling on a hug for my Grandmother.

"I love you Grandmother."

"And I you, little Olson."

**Atlantis Rises**

**Captain's Log 13.81 Earth Years After Bang**

There is no going back and I've had to live with that for nearly 1 million years. The Seraphim gave us Atlantians this covenant for immortality among the stars. Atlantians had been chosen to move beyond the atmosphere and join this angelic race of intergalactic nomads. The rest of the humans on Earth were left behind to their own devices. In return for joining our society with theirs, we'd be able to migrate across an unknowable universe, be given the secrets to immortality, and timeless bodies that never sickened.

Even so, it was not a choice made lightly.

The Council deliberated on it for a full year before all was said and done. My own family was split on the subject. I'd argued that we are not responsible for the world but others...felt differently. Finally, it was decided, those who wished to remain were given all they could carry, but those who wished to go were given the city of Atlantis itself. Every arching spire and twisting canal were covered in a vast dome. Construction was immense and fiercely pursued. Once completed, Atlantis was raised from the ground and lifted into the stars by the Seraphim leaving a crater filled by the ocean.

*I vividly recall watching my twin sister staring up at our domed city from the shoreline. Her green eyes are vibrant against her charcoal skin. The sun setting cast a long shadow from her rapidly diminishing form as I ascended with the city. But most of all I recall her face. A face filled with spite as I left her to join the Seraphim. I'd begged her to come but she acted so foolishly. I did not understand how she could choose to remain a leftover on Earth after everything we'd seen together. I still struggle with her choice.*

*The cost of leaving my world behind was a steep one. Suns do not rise and fall in the ether of space. Simply knowing I'll never see it from the vibrant green hills of Earth haunts me. Throughout every passing age with each new strange world, I've visited that haunting visage grows. The lifeless planets far outnumber those with life like I'd left behind. It hurts to know that so many worlds are missing this miracle that changes and balances a world. I never expected the universe to be so empty.*

*So perhaps that is why I've broken the one rule I've been given.*

*Let this Captain's log be a record of my misdeeds once the Seraphim finally track me down. I left*

*Atlantis domed spaceport in a stolen Seraphim shuttle and have returned to my old world. I think I just wanted to see the sunrise there once more.*

*Now I wish I'd not returned.*

*Memory is such an imperfect thing. We shape it in ways that distort reality. When a dream is finally measured against its origin that distortion becomes apparent. Standing on this Earth, it is not the one I remember. After so many lifeless worlds I'd expected to see the grassy hills of the Earth. I'd forgotten that things could die and so much has died here.*

*The sun rises over not the green hills but over a sea of trash. It rises over a wasteland and waters polluted to the point they're more red than blue. The plants die underneath this flood of waste and the balance of nature has been overcome by the leftover humanity's numerous population. This...this is why I left! Humanity can't be trusted left to its own devices. It breeds destruction and-*

"Hey, Lady!" The voice is translated by my teardrop earring and I turn to a bizarre sight. A small dark-skinned woman wearing blue jeans overalls is scowling at me with her hands on her hips. My breath catches as my eyes meet her vibrant green ones.

"Yenna?" I whisper as my mind floods me back to 950,000 years ago. Me standing on the edge of a city on the rise and my sister glaring up at me as I leave her and the rest of the leftovers behind. An uneasy feeling grabs my stomach I'd not felt in ages, guilt has ahold of me.

"What? No, my name is Maria." The short woman gives me a confused glance. Her brow furrowing and eyebrow arching judgmentally, "Look lady you seem a bit lost so let me help you out. You're in the middle of a cleanup. I'm going to have to ask you to leave unless you want to stick around and help out."

She jokingly waves a hand at a spare bucket and a pair of pincers. Behind her, I notice, for the first time, more people scattered around the waste and sorting it into separate piles. The momentous effort was taken on bit by bit with the volunteers behind her. Behind them, the sun is finally fully risen over the horizon. They're still here. The leftovers are still here and still trying against insurmountable odds.

"Why do you even bother?" I ask Maria.

Her playful demeanor changes and all that's left is the scorn, "Because, this is my home so you are leaving or what?"

I look back at her and the sunset that frames her face. This isn't the world I remembered but that doesn't mean I can't find it again. I go to pick up the bucket, "I-I'm going to stay."

"Good." A slow smile creeps over her face, "We're going to need all the help we can get."

# The Interactive

Hello Reader! Thank you so much for reading my stories. They were inspired by a year long prompt challenge in 2020, each of which are listed below.

If you like what I do subscribe to my https://www.reddit.com/r/LaughingBriar/ subreddit or visit my website https://laughingbriarbooks.com/.

You can send me a prompt and/or write with me online during my monthly prompt challenge. Either way, have a good one stranger.

Noir Fantasy

[WP] The narrator says it's a noir detective story, and refuses to budge

Dragontine

[WP] Extrovert is forced to stay at home alone for 3 months

The Fool's Rush

[WP] While prospecting for gold, you come across an odd crystal which, upon touch, absorbs itself into your skin with intense pain

Tree Lovers

[WP] Couple with members of a diff sentient species (idk, fairies and humans, demons and angels) being introduced to the other person's parents for the first time

## A Bubbly Baby Boy
[WP] Through some strange quirk of genetics, a child with gills is born to two parents without them. Neither of them was prepared for this possibility.

## Gleaver's Travels
[WP] You wake up surrounded by a tribe of diminutive...frog-people...it would be cute, but you are bound. What are the frog-people's plans?

## The Dragon Prince
[WP] You're a courier in a fantasy world. You are delivering a package from the human kingdom to the elf kingdom when you're ambushed by dragons and you discover you are the reincarnated dragon prince, they have some tasks for you that you weren't expecting.

## Fruit of the Lute
[WP] You're abducted by weird aliens who feed off of sound but don't understand spoken language. This leads to an issue when it comes to feeding you.

## The Temple of Ayie

[WP] The key to human happiness has been figured out by an AI. You were guaranteed to live a happy and fulfilling life, provided you agreed to follow its every order without question. One day, the AI gives you the order to destroy it.

## Personal Holographic Interface

[WP] You live in an advanced society where most people have a PHI - a Personal Holographic Intelligence - who help manage aspects of your life. After the latest update, they all become sentient.

## Saturn's Wisdom

[WP] You're 100 years old, and the venerated elder of a post-apocalyptic stone-age tribe. As the last blood kin and descendant of Generation Z, who witnessed the end days on the "world wide web", you have been tasked with passing on the stories of the ancients to the next generation.

## Reflections of a Transporter

[WP] Your crew moves hazardous items or creatures, only the most dangerous. Next item is a mirror. The hazard is "it shows you who you truly are."

## Captain of Shipwrecks

[WP] The Captain of shipwrecks

## Atlantis Rises

[WP] Standard practice is to uplift the most advanced group and leave the rest in place indefinitely as a preserve

Feeling Inspired? Write your
story here:

_____

_____

_____

_____

_____

_____

_____

_____

_____

120

Made in the USA
Middletown, DE
14 October 2023